ROSIE REINDEER
and the
CHRISTMAS WISH

Rosie is a reindeer if nobody knows she's called Rosie because of her nose

Related to Rudolph, her famous cousin
there are many of them, more than a dozen

She didn't worry about dark or night
her little red nose shone ever so bright

"Oh Rosie please help us the winter is bleak,
I can't seem to see the trees or the street"

So she held her head high and led the way,
what a nice reindeer to save the day!

But Rosie wished that it was Christmas already
so she packed up a snack, her blanket and teddy

"I'm off to the forest to find some cheer
to make sure we have a happy end to the year"

Off she went to her favourite spot
under the stars that were tiny dots

"Oh glittery stars you look like wishes,
please hear mine" as she blew them kisses

"We need some magic very badly
so we can end the year less sadly"

"I wish that everyone has fun
and chocolate, cakes and sticky buns

Toys and tinsel and lovely cuddles
let no one be sad or in a muddle"

She wished and wished as hard as could be
then snuggled up against a tree

"I must stay awake and wish some more
so no one is lonely or sad anymore"

But it was very late and Rosie laid down under the trees on the wintery ground

"We heard you little deer, the stars did say and you shall have your Christmas Day"

"Time to share with the people you enjoy,
food and games and lots of toys"

"You care so much about everyone
it's time for you to have some fun

We'll make it snow so you can play
and build a snowman on Christmas Day"

Something cold fell upon Rosie's nose
she wiggled her head and bottom and toes

"It's snowing, it's snowing" Rosie said
as she danced about with her favourite ted

"It must be Christmas Day right now
I must run back to my snowy town"

When she got there, she could see
everyone around their trees

"Merry Christmas everyone
and thank you stars"

"For a special day that's truly ours"

We hope you enjoyed Rosie's festive adventure!

For more information about Imajica Theatre go to

IMAJICATHEATRE.CO.UK

Printed in Great Britain
by Amazon

85211223R00018